Tinkling

a Treasure Troll Tale

Stephen Cosgrove

illustrated by
Diana Rice Bonin

A Golden Book • New York
Western Publishing Company, Inc., Racine, Wisconsin 53404

The Carousel ® ™
13110 NE 177th PL
Woodinville, WA 98072

Publisher: Nancy L. Cosgrove
Business Director: Terri Anderson
Creative Editor: Matt Stuart

Tinkling
a Treasure Troll Tale by Stephen Cosgrove

Treasure Trolls concept and development © 1991 Carousel,
International, Inc.
Treasure Trolls © 1992 Ace Novelty. All other trademarks are
the property of Western Publishing Company, Inc. Library of
Congress Number: 92-72511 ISBN 0-307-13451-2
A MCMXCII

Dedicated to Matt Stuart and the Attkisson family, all of whom live in the land of Hodge Podge. Unfortunately, there is one Matt Stuart and lebinty-billion Attkissons and if I named them all by name there wouldn't have been room for the book. Thank you for being you.

Stephen

Magic is here – for this is the land of Hodge Podge and the village of Hairst Bree. In this land and in this village live fairylike creatures called Treasure Trolls. Their laughter tinkles like crystal bells as they scamper about searching for magical little jewels called WishStones. For every troll knows that when you wish upon a WishStone all your dreams come true. When a WishStone is found, the Treasure Troll who finds it can wish upon it. All he or she needs to say is,

"TINKLE, TWINKLE, HAIR SO FUZZY.
TINKLE, TWINKLE, BEES GO BUZZY.
WISH I MAY,
WISH I MIGHT
HAVE THE WISH I WISH TONIGHT."

And just like that the wishes are granted. Magic is here – in the very hearts of the Treasure Trolls and in the WishStones they carry.

The Wil 'O Wisp Mountains are a magical place where the creatures of Hodge Podge roam free. It is here that the woolly chipmunks frolic in the spring after being sheared of their woolly winter coats. Here the twitters, birds of another feather, flock together in the tangled gnarlwood trees, singing odd little melodies that echo throughout the woods. Here there are trollbears that lumber and troll-bunnies that hop about the mountain meadows in peace and harmony.

Most special of all are the sequins, delightful tiny unicorns whose single horns glitter in sparkling opalescence. They would rear on their tiny legs and race down forest paths and rustic roads. The sequins are the freest of the creatures that roam the Wil 'O Wisp Mountains. They all live here. They all play here. The land of Hodge Podge is their home.

There are more than just wild creatures in the mountains and meadows of Hodge Podge. For here also live the Treasure Trolls. Once the Treasure Trolls believed they held dominion over all the land. They thought that just because the land was there, it was theirs for the taking.

Over the years the Treasure Trolls had built rustic cabins, cottages, barns, and other farm buildings. Nature's paths that once wound freely throughout the land now ended abruptly at fences of Knobbily Pine and walls of river rock.

The Treasure Trolls were proud of all they built. They were prouder still of their fruit and vegetable gardens. To grow their fruits and vegetables, the trolls had plowed and furrowed the rolling meadows until they were as flat as flat could be. The trolls grew carrots and lettuce, rich in the sweetness of the land. They planted rows and rows of fruit trees that produced the juiciest of apples and pears and plums. Near the orchards they planted shrubs that grew sun-soaked trollberries – ripened sweet on prickly vines.

All was abundant and all was good on the farms of the Treasure Trolls.

But amid all of this abundance there was a problem. In order to produce more fruits and vegetables, the Treasure Trolls had to remove most of the natural vegetation. They plowed and turned under meadows of sweet clover and wild wheat. They burned the tangled thickets of Treasure Berry. They chopped to firewood the groves of Sun Plum and Crabapple. They destroyed what grew wild and free, taking away what had been food for the free creatures of the forest. Meadow after meadow was transformed into farmland.

No creatures had eaten more of the wild foods of the meadows than the sequins. As their food sources diminished, they moved higher into the mountains, where there seemed to be plenty. But as time went on, all the wild meadows were replaced by farms. There were few natural foods to eat. The sequins were a herd of unicorns with nowhere to live and nothing to eat.

Less hungry than some and more hungry than others was a pretty little sequin called Tinkling. She was called Tinkling for her tiny hooves that rang likc bells as she trotted on the stream stones that bedded the forest paths.

One day Tinkling trotted down a path that she hadn't run in years. The path twisted and turned through the forest, ending abruptly at the edge of a Treasure Troll farm. Tinkling's first thought was to run back into the forest. But the farm smelled of ripe fruit and she was so very hungry.

Hesitantly, Tinkling stepped from the forest and began to nibble on a trollberry, ripe on the vine. She ate one, she ate two, and then she ate many. Soon she was eating all of the fruits and vegetables on the farm. She ate the carrots that crackled and snapped. She slurped the sweetness of the berries. All was delight. All was delicious.

With her tummy filled, Tinkling hurried to gather the herd and bring them back to this oasis of food in an otherwise barren land. So full was she, her tiny hooves did not tinkle – they clanged.

Tinkling brought the whole herd of starving sequins back to the farm. There they all ate to their hearts' content. Each one ate only a little, but as a herd they ate a lot. Fulfilled, they danced about the fields, horns flashing in the light. Cloven hooves kicked in the air in total delight of the finished banquet and the anticipation of meals to come.

But even on the sunniest days, clouds can swell and darken the horizon. So it was with the storm gathering over the cottage at the edge of the farm.

Standing on the porch, their hands shading the bright sun to better see the sequins in the field, was a Treasure Troll family – Triska, Trousers, and their daughter, Joy. They were not happy, for this was their farm and the sequins were eating all of their fruits and vegetables.

"They must stop," grumbled Father Trousers.
"They have no right," mumbled Mother Triska.
Joy said nothing. She simply watched in wonder. . .

The very next day, as the sun lazily stretched over Mount Wishbone, Triska and Trousers built a fence. Even more of the forest was ripped down as ancient gnarlwood and Knobbily Pine became a fine, tall fence that circled the farm, dotted with gates here and there. They built it strong. They built it well. Now their farm and gardens would be safe from the sequins.

As her parents worked, little Joy simply watched in wonder. Not far away, hidden in the wind-strewn leaves of smoky elm, Tinkling, too, watched in wonder.

The following day, when it was time to eat, the sequins returned to the farm. There, as Tinkling had warned, was the fence built by Triska and Trousers, the farming Treasure Trolls. The sequins milled about, nervous and afraid. Nervous about the fence and afraid they would soon be hungry again.

Tinkling's hooves were ringing like the singing of silver bells as she ran along the fence, looking for a place to enter. Finally she turned and raced from the fence. Spinning in a flurry of leaves and ground debris, she turned and, at a full gallop, ran straight at the fence.

Nearby, Joy watched the little unicorn. She caught her breath as Tinkling raced toward the fence, sure the little sequin was about to crash. Then, like magic, the sequin leaped from the ground and silkily soared into the air. She jumped the fence as if she had wings. Within moments other sequins followed and the air seemed filled with unicorn butterflies fluttering over the fence.

Triska and Trousers were so angry that they even tried to use their WishStones to wish the sequins away. But wishes that would hurt a fellow troll or any other living creature are never granted, so nothing happened.

Frustrated, Trousers ran into the cottage and grabbed the rope that he kept hanging on the door. He made a large loop that he twirled over his head as he raced down the steps of the porch out into the garden. The rope twirled and twirled as he tossed it like a spinning snake above the heads of the grazing sequins. The rope settled like a wreath around Tinkling's neck. Trousers cinched the rope tight. He turned and said with a smile, "Well, I got one. . ."

That was all he said before Tinkling realized she was caught. Her eyes opened wide. She gulped once and took off with a gallop for the safety of the forest. Trousers foolishly held on to the rope and was dragged, bouncing, across the garden.

Tinkling leaped – and even dragging the troll behind – she cleared the gate.

Unfortunately, Trousers didn't do the same. He hit the gate with such force that the fence fell over. There he lay in a daze, muttering, "Well, I got one. . . I got one. . . I got one. . ."

Joy and her mother, Triska, rushed to Trousers as he lay in the wreckage of the fallen fence. They helped him to his feet, freeing a carrot that some-how had become stuck in his ear.

"Uhhmm," Trousers grumbled angrily. "I am going to set a trap for those awful little sequins and then we will see who drags *who* to where."

"Wait, Poppa," said Joy. "Let me find the sequins. I'll tell them they must stay away. I am sure they mean no harm."

With her parents' reluctant permission, Joy carefully stepped through the debris of the fence and entered the forest, the shrinking domain of the sequins.

Joy wandered in the forest, but nowhere could she find the mysterious unicorns. As she searched, she heard a bell-like tinkling. She turned this way and that but could not find the source of the sound. After a time, she stopped beside a crystal water pool and knelt to take a drink. She looked down into the water and was surprised to see the reflection of a sequin looking back at her.

Careful not to spook this gentle creature, Joy sat up, turned, and looked it in the eye. She waited and the sequin waited. They both waited and waited.

Resolved that she would speak first, Joy said softly, "My name is Joy and I am a Treasure Troll. You have been stealing the vegetables from our garden. Although you are of great wonder to me, you will have to stop stealing. If you don't stop stealing, my father will trap you and he will cause you great harm."

There was a silence and then the sequin whispered, "My name is Tinkling and we are not stealing. We are only taking that which was taken from us. Before you came, our land was free and laden with good things to eat. You have taken the land. You have taken our food. We are only taking back a part of that which was taken from us."

Joy had no argument. The sequin was right. But how could both sequin and troll live in the land?

Oh, what a dilemma! But from great questions come great answers. Joy thought. Tinkling thought. They thought together.

Ah, there was the answer – together. They would work – together. They would share the land – together.

They rushed back to the farm. With the herd of sequins watching from the open field, Tinkling and Joy told Trousers and Triska their exciting solution to the problem.

At first the grown-up Treasure Trolls were a bit skeptical, as are most adults when a child solves an adult-sized problem. But soon they both realized that Joy and Tinkling were right. Together they had thought of the only solution.

So it came to be in the land of Hodge Podge that Treasure Trolls helped the sequins and the magical unicorns helped the trolls. Triska and Trousers built little barns where the sequins slept in shelter from the storms. The plowing and planting were much easier with the aid of the sequins, who thought it great fun to work side by side with the trolls throughout the day.

At nighttime, when the moon was full and bright, the sequins danced in the starlight as Triska, Trousers and Joy sat singing on the porch,

"DANCE, LITTLE TINKLING, DANCE.
DANCE, LITTLE TINKLING, DANCE.
YOUR HOOVES DO SING,
LIKE BELLS THAT RING.
DANCE, LITTLE TINKLING, DANCE."

And dance she did, and dance she does in the light of the silvery moon.

Now, all the Treasure Trolls are wishing on their WishStones that your wishes will come true, too.

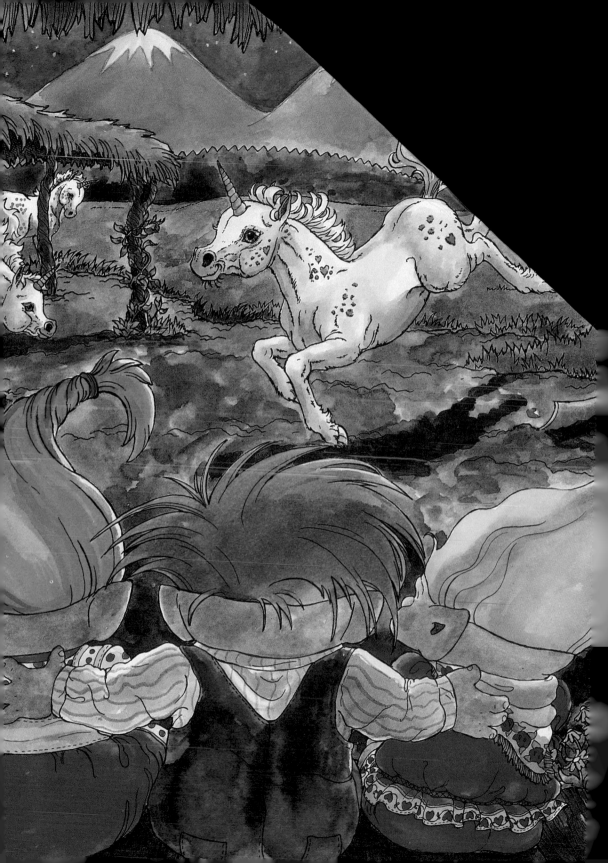

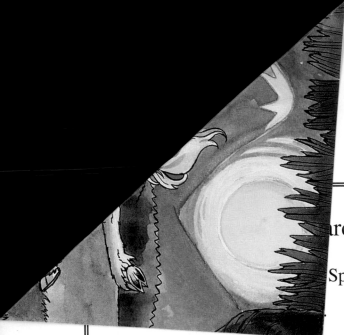

rd Cosgrove

Spokane, Washington.

...has written and published over two hundred children's titles.

...lives now with his beloved wife Nancy, his delightful stepson Matthew, his little dog Rhubarb, Snickers the attack cat and two goldfish the size of whales in the foothills just outside Seattle, Washington.

Stephen Edward Cosgrove

...was born July 26, 1945, in Spokane, Washington.

...was raised in Boise, Idaho.

...has written and published over two hundred children's titles.

...lives now with his beloved wife Nancy, his delightful stepson Matthew, his little dog Rhubarb, Snickers the attack cat and two goldfish the size of whales in the foothills just outside Seattle, Washington.